Cezar's Pollution Solution

by Kelli Luce
illustrated by Louise Ellis

 HOUGHTON MIFFLIN HARCOURT
School Publishers

Printed in China

ISBN-13: 978-0-547-01732-7
ISBN-10: 0-547-01732-4

4 5 6 7 8 0940 18 17 16 15 14 13 12 11 10

One Monday morning, Cezar's teacher, Ms. Rosco, introduced a new DVD.

"This might be the most important movie I've ever shown you," Ms. Rosco said. "It's about global warming."

Cezar had heard about global warming, but he didn't really understand it. Supposedly, the Earth was getting warmer. But now it was the first week of December, and it was cold outside. Just that morning, the TV weather report had said a big snowstorm would hit town later in the week. So how could it be getting warmer?

As Ms. Rosco set up the DVD player, Cezar looked out the window. Winter was his favorite season, and he couldn't wait for the snow.

The movie opened with a scene that showed cars causing air pollution. Then it showed the ice caps melting in the Arctic. The melting ice caused polar bears to lose some of their habitat.

The woman in the film explained that some scientists believe air pollution is slowly warming the atmosphere. As the temperature rises, Earth might experience extreme changes in the climate. Some areas might stop getting snow.

"Oh, no," Cezar thought. "No snow?"

But then the woman in the film said it wasn't too late to solve the problem.

The movie had hardly finished playing when Cezar's hand shot up.

"This all sounds complicated," Cezar said. "What can a bunch of fourth graders do to stop the world's weather from changing?"

"That's a great question, Cezar," Ms. Rosco said. "Follow me."

Ms. Rosco led the class to the cafeteria. There, they met Mr. Black.

"We create a lot of waste here in the cafeteria," Mr. Black said. "We recycle it. But trucks still have to bring that waste to the landfill. They burn a lot of fuel. Less garbage would mean fewer trips to the landfill, and less pollution. That's why we thought of the Great Pollution Solution contest."

Ms. Rosco held up a poster announcing the contest. The rules were simple. Students in each grade would think of ways to recycle rubbish from the cafeteria. Whoever did the most creative recycling project in each class would win a prize—a brand new Rocket Racer sled. The sleds were given to the school by a local toy store that wanted to help save the environment.

Cezar couldn't believe it. He had always wanted a Rocket Racer!

Mr. Black led the kids back to the rubbish storage area.

"Here's the trash," Mr. Black said. "Your challenge is to come up with an interesting way to reuse this stuff."

There was a pile of bent old silverware. There were heaps of empty milk cartons. Dripping bags of vegetable peels filled the rubbish bin, too.

Cezar spotted a pile of old cafeteria trays.

"Now those look like something I can use," he thought.

The next day, Cezar's class began to work on their projects. Some of the kids worked in teams. Cezar wanted to work on his own. He wanted the Rocket Racer all to himself!

Cezar put up a big piece of cardboard and marked it TOP SECRET. Then he took the cafeteria trays and began to work behind the cardboard wall.

Meanwhile, Sara's team decided to make something out of rinsed-out milk cartons. Armond's team decided to recycle the old, bent silverware. Ollie's team chose the weirdest material of all. They brought in a bucket of rotten vegetable peels.

Cezar worked hard, but by the end of the first day, the only idea he had was using the trays as hats to provide shade from the sun. Unfortunately, the hats kept falling off his head.

On the second day, Sara's team finished its project. Sara explained their idea. "As you know, milk cartons usually get thrown away. But we figured out a 'comfortable' way to use them."

Cezar thought that sounded silly. Comfortable? Milk cartons?

Sara took the cover off a small model that the team had built.

"We call it the Carton Couch," Paco said. "It's cool furniture that you can put in your home."

Cezar had to admit the Carton Couch looked kind of cool.

Cezar thought and thought, but he still couldn't think of any good ways to use the cafeteria trays. The best thing he came up with was turning them into bookshelves.

Now Cezar started to worry. Only two days remained in the contest. He needed a new idea—fast!

Cezar lay awake that night, trying to think of a new idea. No ideas came.

The next morning, Armond's team showed off its Pollution Solution.

"This old silverware was too bent to use in the cafeteria," said Armond. "So we used it to make jewelry. We call it Silver Wear!"

The bracelets and necklaces looked fantastic. Even Ms. Rosco tried one on. That made Cezar worry even more. Two teams had come up with great ideas. How could he come up with something better?

That day, Cezar came up with a new idea. He called it the TrayChair. The TrayChair looked great, but when Cezar sat on it, the chair fell apart, and Cezar landed on the floor.

Then Ollie announced that his team was ready to show off its Pollution Solution.

"Remember the slimy vegetable peels? We're using them to make our new product—Flower Power Compost."

"We took the vegetable peels and put them in a bucket," Carolyn said. "We added a little soil, some dry straw, and some worms."

"We got the worms from the fishing store," said Ollie. "In a few weeks, the peels will turn into really rich food for house plants or gardens."

"Disgusting!" said Cezar.

"Not really," said Ms. Rosco. "I could use some in my garden this spring."

Cezar started getting really nervous. He brought some of the trays home so he could work on an idea that night. But he couldn't think of anything.

When Cezar walked to school the next morning, the ground was covered with snow. Snow usually made him happy. This time, it only made him mad.

"I'll never win that Rocket Racer!" he said to himself. He felt so bad that he took one of the cafeteria trays and flung it across the yard. It slid all the way to the house next door.

"Wow!" Cezar thought. "That tray really moves!" That's when he got the idea.

Cezar ran all the way to school. He got the rest of his trays. Then he asked the school janitor, Ms. Larson, to punch holes in the trays and to cut two long pieces of rope for him.

Cezar put everything together. He ran the rope Ms. Larson had given him through the holes in the trays. Then he tied the rope ends together.

He was just in time, too.

"Well, Cezar," said Ms. Rosco. "You're the only one who hasn't shared an idea for the contest. Anything to show us today?"

Cezar laid out his solution in front of the class. It looked like a train made of trays.

"It's called a TrayBoggan. But I really have to show you how it works outside."

"All right, class," said Ms. Rosco. "Everyone bundle up, and we'll let Cezar show us how his TrayBoggan works."

Cezar put his TrayBoggan down on the snow in the playground. He invited a few classmates to sit on it. Then Cezar began pulling them. The TrayBoggan glided over the snow. It worked like a charm!

All through recess, the kids took turns riding on the TrayBoggan. Everyone loved it—even Ms. Rosco.

In fact, the TrayBoggan was so much fun, Cezar and the rest of the class forgot all about the Rocket Racer sled.

Responding

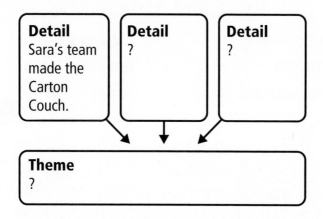

✔ **TARGET SKILL** **Author's Purpose** Story details give clues about the theme, or main point, that an author wants you to know. Copy and complete the chart below to tell about the theme in this book.

Detail
Sara's team made the Carton Couch.

Detail
?

Detail
?

Theme
?

✏ Write About It

Text to World Write a letter to your town newspaper persuading people to do more recycling. Give at least three reasons why more recycling would help the environment.

✓ **TARGET SKILL** **Author's Purpose** Use text details to tell why an author writes a book.

✓ **TARGET STRATEGY** **Monitor/Clarify** As you read, find a way to clear up what doesn't make sense to you.

GENRE **Humorous fiction** is a story that is written to entertain the reader.